What can we grow?

T0337063

Written by Mary Roulston

Illustrated by Chloe Evans

Collins

What's in this book?

Listen and say 🎧①

Download the audio at www.collins.co.uk/839683

trees

flowers

The families look at the garden.

The families are planting vegetables. They plant carrot and bean seeds in the ground. They plant potatoes, too.

They are planting tomatoes in a greenhouse. The tomatoes aren't cold in there.

greenhouse

seeds

The children are planting flowers.
They want bees and butterflies in
the garden.

They plant a lot of flower seeds.

9

What are these?

They are fruit trees. They grow apples and pears. The trees have got flowers on them now.

Sun and water is good for the garden.

The families don't want rabbits and birds to eat the baby vegetables.

13

They love being in the garden.

The vegetables and flowers are growing very tall!

Look at the flowers now! What colours can you see?

There are lots of bees and butterflies on the flowers.

17

Look at the carrots, beans and potatoes!

The tomatoes in the greenhouse are red now. There are small apples and pears on the trees.

The families are having lunch.

They are eating the fruit and vegetables from the garden!

Picture dictionary

Listen and repeat

butterfly

greenhouse

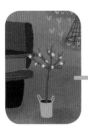

grow

plant

rabbit

vegetables

1 Look and say "Yes" or "No"

The tomatoes are cold in the greenhouse.

These are vegetable trees.

Water is good for plants.

The flowers are very small.

2 Listen and say

Collins

Published by Collins
An imprint of HarperCollins*Publishers*
Westerhill Road
Bishopbriggs
Glasgow
G64 2QT

HarperCollins*Publishers*
1st Floor, Watermarque Building
Ringsend Road
Dublin 4
Ireland

William Collins' dream of knowledge for all began with the publication of his first book in 1819.

A self-educated mill worker, he not only enriched millions of lives, but also founded a flourishing publishing house. Today, staying true to this spirit, Collins books are packed with inspiration, innovation and practical expertise. They place you at the centre of a world of possibility and give you exactly what you need to explore it.

© HarperCollins*Publishers* Limited 2020

10 9 8 7 6 5 4 3 2

ISBN 978-0-00-839683-1

Collins® and COBUILD® are registered trademarks of HarperCollins*Publishers* Limited

www.collins.co.uk/elt

British Library Cataloguing in Publication Data

A catalogue record for this publication is available from the British Library.

Author: Mary Roulston
Illustrator: Chloe Evans (Beehive)
Series editor: Rebecca Adlard
Commissioning editor: Zoë Clarke
Publishing manager: Lisa Todd
Product managers: Jennifer Hall and Caroline Green
In-house editor: Alma Puts Keren
Project manager: Emily Hooton
Editor: Emma Wilkinson
Proofreaders: Natalie Murray and Michael Lamb
Cover designer: Kevin Robbins
Typesetter: 2Hoots Publishing Services Ltd
Audio produced by id audio, London
Reading guide author: Emma Wilkinson
Production controller: Rachel Weaver
Printed and bound by: GPS Group, Slovenia

MIX
Paper from
responsible sources

FSC
www.fsc.org
FSC™ C007454

Download the audio for this book and a reading guide for parents and teachers at www.collins.co.uk/839683